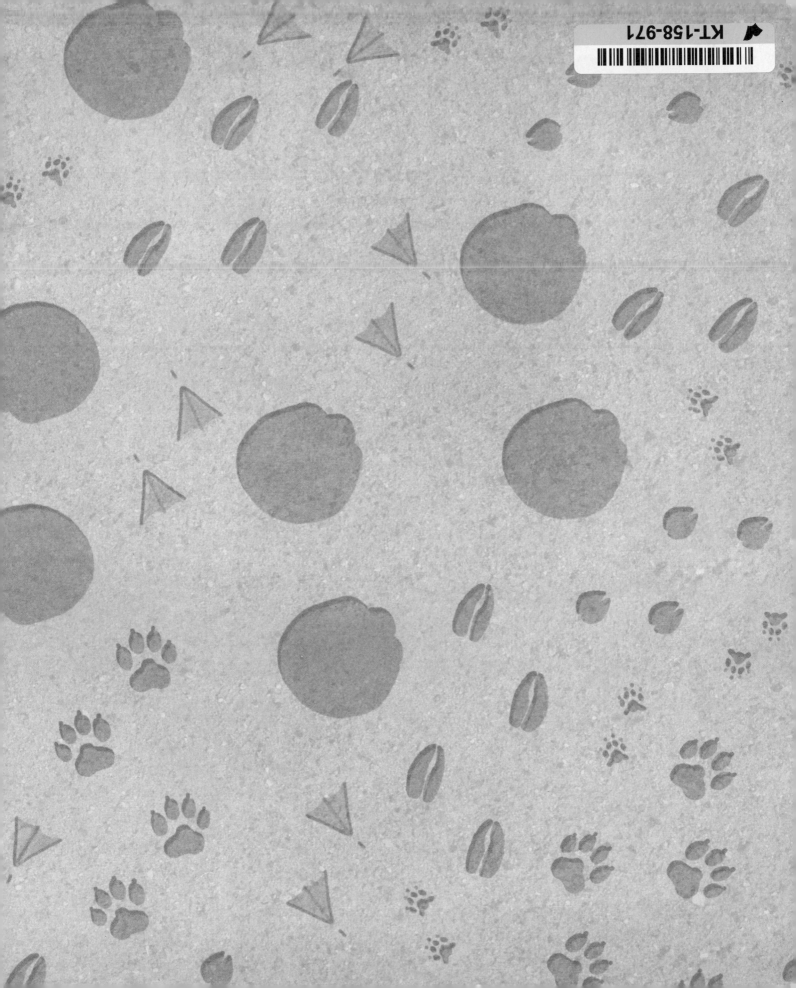

For Alexander Kwon and Gi Cho   S.J.D.

To my "little meerkat" Tommaso – like Miki,
he is coming out of his burrow to get to know the world!   G.C.

Text copyright © 2015 Sarah J. Dodd
Illustrations copyright © 2015 Giusi Capizzi
This edition copyright © 2015 Lion Hudson

The right of Sarah J. Dodd to be identified as the author and of Giusi Capizzi to be identified as the illustrator of
this work has been asserted by them in accordance with the Copyright, Designs and Patents Act 1988.

Published by Lion Children's Books
an imprint of
Lion Hudson plc
Wilkinson House, Jordan Hill Road,
Oxford OX2 8DR, England
www.lionhudson.com/lionchildrens

Hardback ISBN 978 0 7459 6597 0
Paperback ISBN 978 0 7459 6598 7

First edition 2015

A catalogue record for this book is available from the British Library

Printed and bound in Malaysia, May 2015, LH18

LEGS

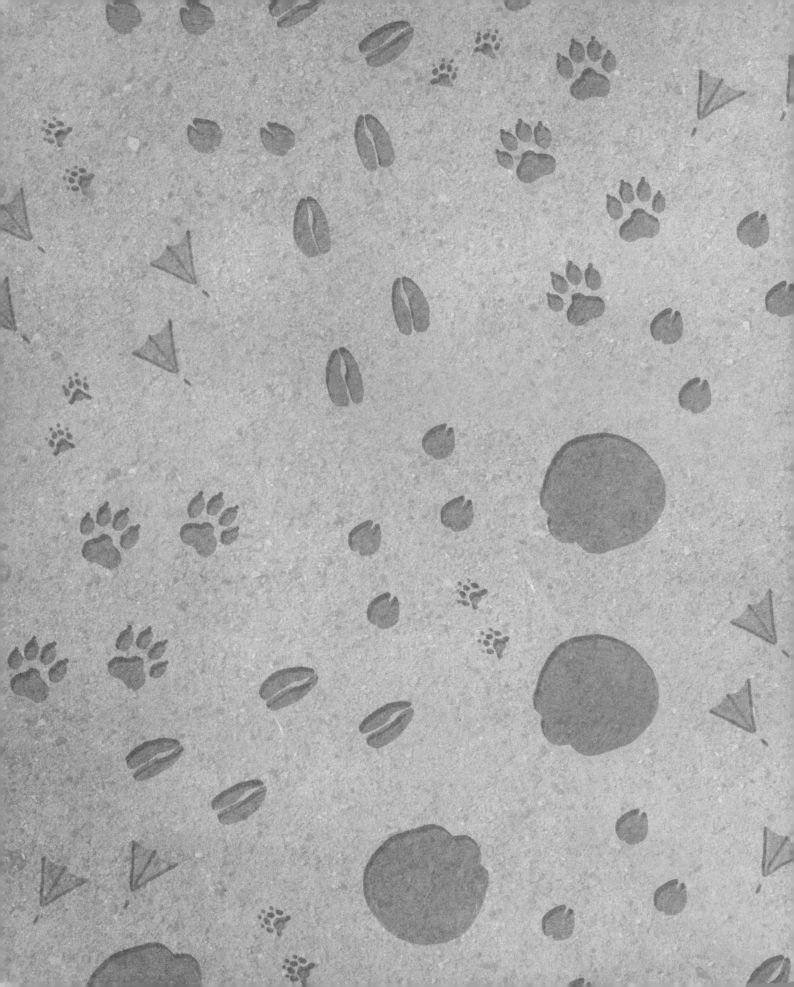

LEGS

The tale of a meerkat
lost and found

Sarah J. Dodd
Illustrated by Giusi Capizzi

LION
CHILDREN'S

Miki and Mama lived under the ground,
where it was warm, dark, and safe.

One day, Miki woke up and Mama was gone.
"Mama?" he said.
But Mama was nowhere to be seen.

"Miki!" called Mama. "Come outside and see the world."
"I don't like outside," said Miki. "I don't want to see the world."

"I'll be here," said Mama, "and the keeper will take
care of us."

Outside, it was light;

it was bright;

it was exciting…

... and a little bit frightening.

But Mama was always there, and the keeper took care of them.

Miki wanted to see more of the world.

But the world was full of LEGS!

Pink legs…

and wrinkly legs…

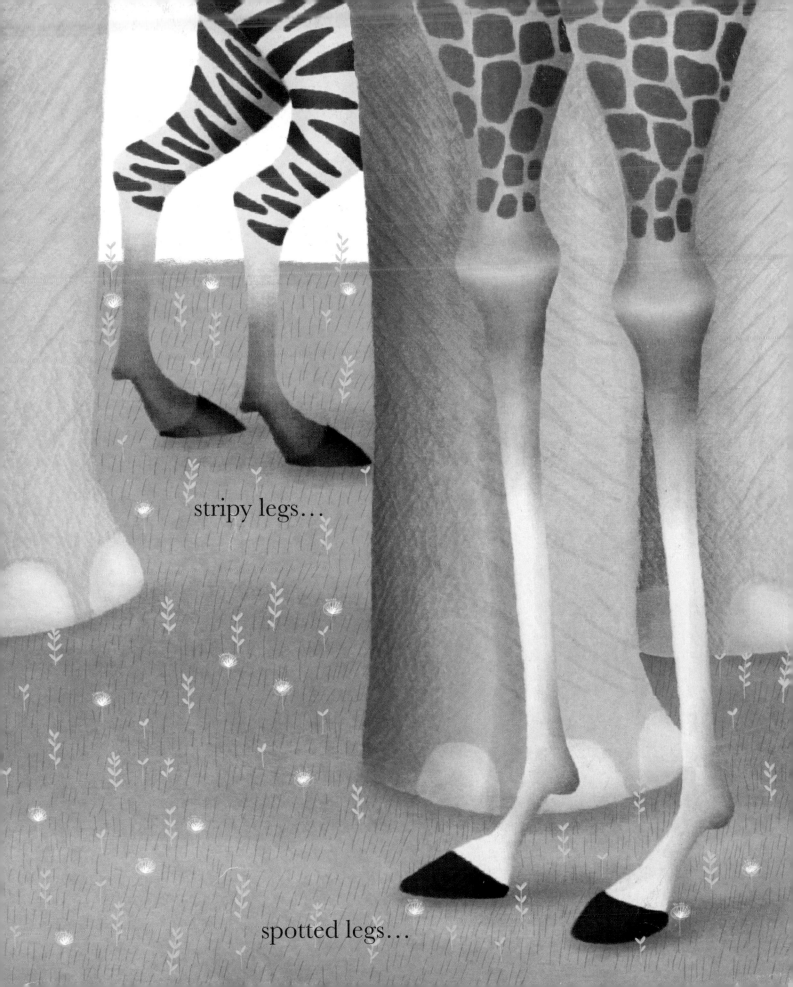

stripy legs…

spotted legs…

… and FIERCE, furry legs that made Miki run as fast as his own little legs would allow.

Outside the zoo, there were even more LEGS of all shapes and sizes…

Even the buildings looked like LEGS, reaching high into the distant sky.

They were *so* tall that Miki felt very, very small.

"MAMA?" said Miki.
But Mama was nowhere to be seen.

"Can I help you, my little friend?"
said a voice.
 Miki knew *those* legs!

But now there were hands as well —
warm and strong, lifting Miki up.

And there was a kind face.

There were faces *everywhere!*

Faces of all shapes and sizes…

FIERCE, furry faces...

stripy faces...

and
spotted faces.

Wrinkly faces...

and pink faces.

And at last…

... the face Miki *loved* best of all.

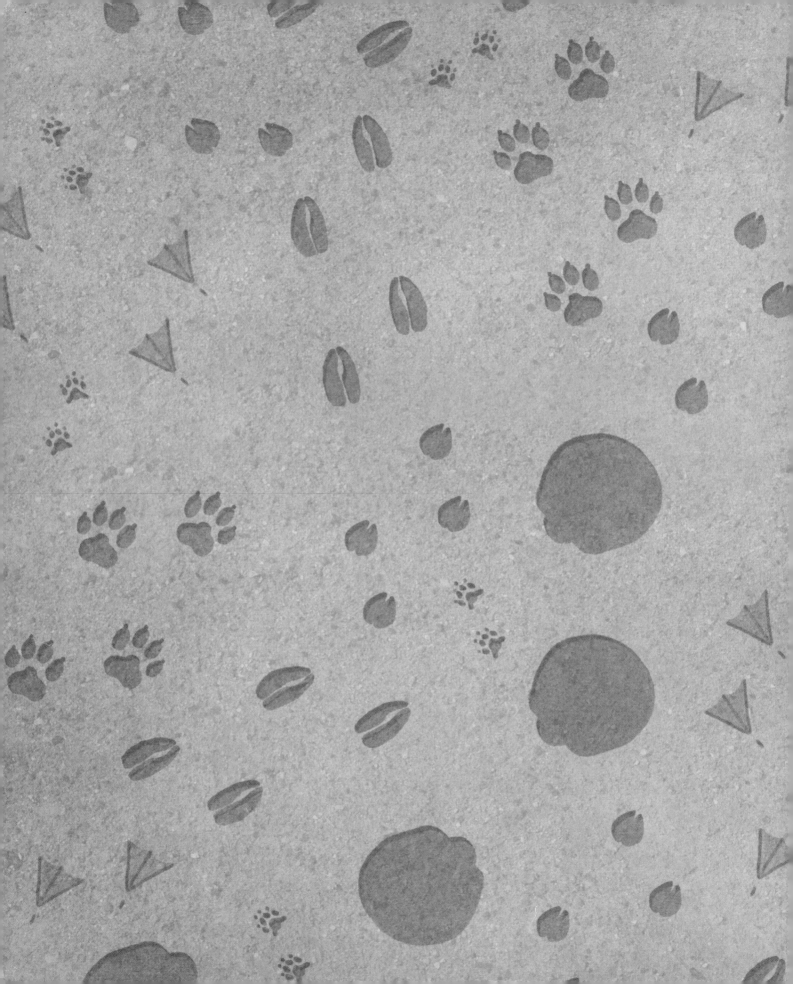

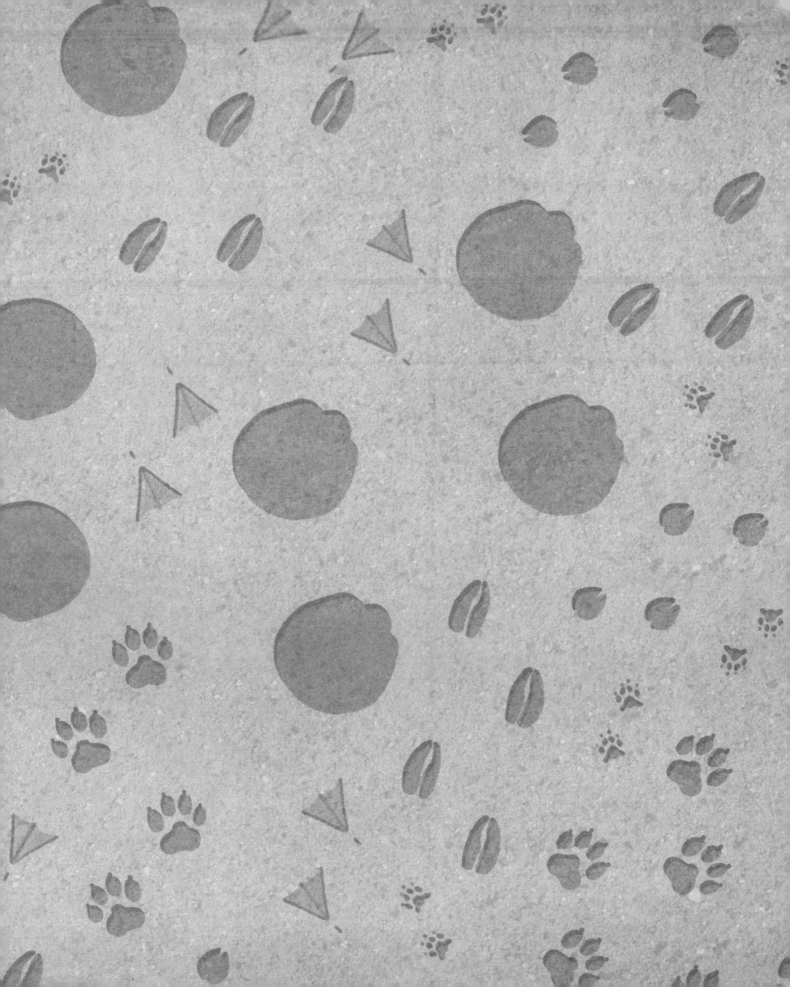

Other titles from Lion Children's Books

Hogs Hate Hugs   *Tiziana Bendall-Brunello & John Bendall-Brunello*

Magnus   *Claire Shorrock*

Missing Jack   *Rebecca Elliott*

Mr Super Poopy Pants   *Rebecca Elliott*

The Sheep in Wolf's Clothing   *Bob Hartman & Tim Raglin*